This book belongs to

Emily   Wicks

For all our great-nephews and nieces
T.B.-B. & J.B.-B.

First published in Great Britain in 2011 by

Gullane Children's Books

185 Fleet Street, London EC2A 4HS

www.gullanebooks.com

This paperback edition first published in 2012.

2 4 6 8 10 9 7 5 3 1

Text © Tiziana Bendall-Brunello 2011
Illustrations © John Bendall-Brunello 2011

The right of John and Tiziana Bendall-Brunello to be identified as the author and illustrator of this work
has been asserted by them, in accordance with the Copyright, Designs and Patents Act, 1988.
A CIP record for this title is available from the British Library.

ISBN: 978-1-86233-813-5

Printed and bound in China

My Favourite Food

Tiziana & John Bendall-Brunello

GULLANE
CHILDREN'S BOOKS

Little Goose and her mummy
were in the yard, enjoying
some fresh, green grass.

'Mmm . . . I love grass,'
said Little Goose. 'It's
my favourite food!

I wonder if everybody loves grass as much as me?'

'Why don't you go and find out,' said Mummy.

So off went Little Goose to find out Pig's favourite food . . .

'What's your favourite food, Pig?'
she asked.

'Apples,'

said Pig. 'They're so juicy!'

'Mmm,' said Little Goose, 'I like apples too.
I wonder what Goat's favourite food is?'

So off she went to find out . . .

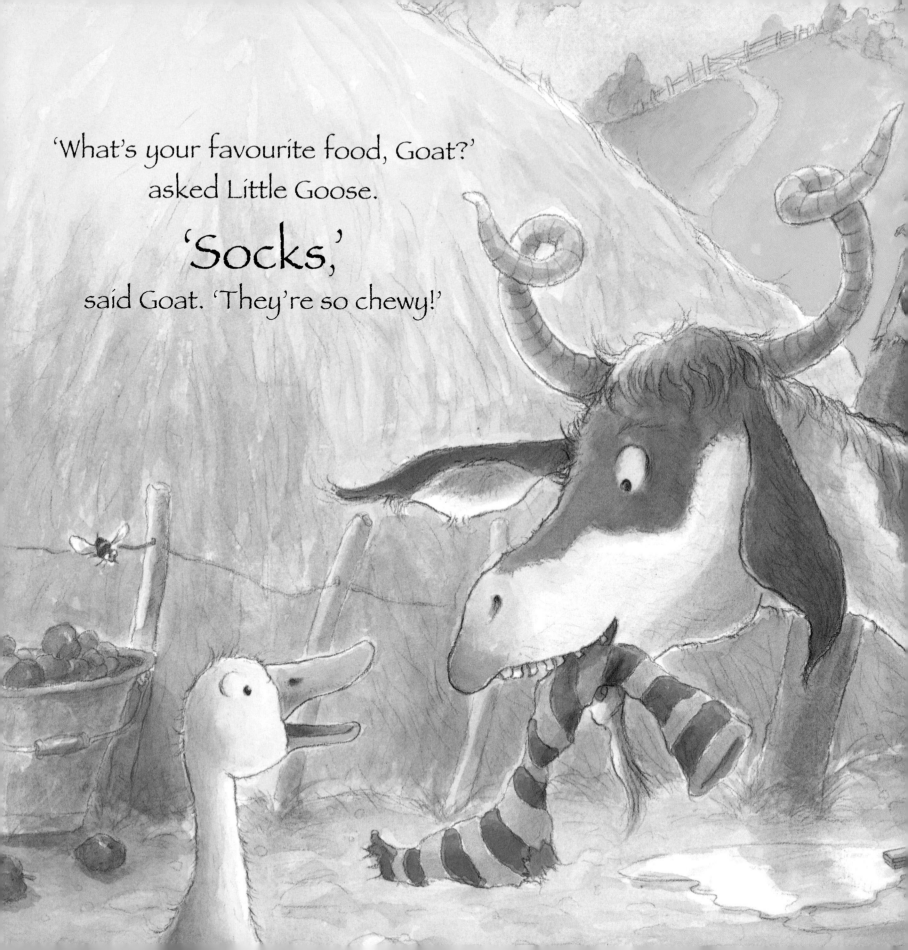

'What's your favourite food, Goat?'
asked Little Goose.

'Socks,'

said Goat. 'They're so chewy!'

'Hmmm,' said Little Goose,
'I'm not sure I like socks!

I wonder what Cow's favourite food is?'

So off she went to find out . . .

'What's your favourite food, Cow?' asked Little Goose.

'Daisies,' said Cow. 'They're so sweet!'

'Mmm,' said Little Goose, 'daisies are tasty.
But I wonder what Fox's
favourite food is?'

So off she went to find out . . .

'Fox! Fox! What's your favourite food?' asked Little Goose.

'Well . . .' said Fox,
'let me think.
My favourite food is . . .'

'YOU!'

'Yikes!' squealed Little Goose.
And she ran away as fast as her
little legs would carry her . . .

. . . safely back into
the loving wings
of her mummy.

And while Little Goose enjoyed some of her
favourite food - grass - Fox chuckled quietly to himself
as he settled down to eat his favourite food . . .

strawberries and cream!